JEWELS OF POWER

Every Word Is A Gem. Every Truth, Holds A Treasure

KAMELAH BLAIR

ISBN: 978-1-998120-84-0

Quote from Victoria:
"They thought the jewels made me powerful—truth is, they carry the weight of everything I've survived."

CHAPTER 1
Red Lips, Real Lies

Victoria stood in front of her mirror, applying the last stroke of matte red lipstick with precision. Each movement calculated. Each layer a mask. Her full lips parted slightly as she admired herself—not out of vanity, but strategy. You didn't survive where she came from without learning how to weaponize beauty.

At 5'5", she moved with the grace of a dancer but the presence of a queen. Her skin, a smooth bronze canvas, glowed against the bathroom's soft lighting. She adjusted her coat collar, eyes narrowing at the shimmering diamond necklace peeking beneath. It wasn't just jewelry. Each piece she wore had a story, a price, a sin.

Tonight, she was headed to The Ember Room, a dimly lit lounge tucked in the heart of the Southside's new development, Sandrow Heights. No one knew she owned it—just the way she liked it. From the outside, it was all velvet ropes and sleek cars. Inside, secrets were traded like currency.

The moment she entered, heads turned. The air shifted. Conversations paused.

"Victoria Starr," someone whispered, as if saying her name too loud might summon ghosts.

She gave a nod to the security at the back—muscle she handpicked—and moved toward the bar. Raven, the bartender, slid her a glass of dark wine without a word.

"You look... lethal," Raven smirked.

"I always do," Victoria replied, eyes scanning the room.

In her purse, she carried a ruby ring—fire red, with edges that sparkled like blood in moonlight. The man who gave it to her never made it to the morning. His name was never important. What mattered was what he knew—and what she made sure he'd never tell.

Her phone buzzed. A name flashed: Unknown.

A text followed.

"I know what the ruby means. Meet me at 11. Carmichael Pier."

Victoria's grip tightened. She slipped the phone into her coat, stood, and left without finishing her wine. There was always someone digging, always someone who didn't know when to stop.

As she disappeared into the night, the ruby pulsed in her palm like it had a heartbeat.

CHAPTER 2
The Necklace

The neon lights of **LuxeBar** reflected off Victoria's heels as she walked into the lounge, a sleek, underground spot tucked away in the **District**—a forgotten corner of the city where the real power brokers played. **LuxeBar** was a name only whispered among those who knew the game. Black leather, gold accents, and dark corners where deals were sealed in silence.

She didn't walk; she *owned* the floor. The click of her heels was a reminder of the power she carried, each step deliberate, each moment a calculated decision. Her eyes scanned the room, taking in the faces of the men and women who could be useful to her, or a threat.

She wore the ruby necklace tonight—the first jewel she had earned. Not by chance, but by carefully orchestrated moves in a world that demanded perfection. As she walked past the bar, she caught the eyes of a few interested parties. But Victoria wasn't here for their attention. She was here for something—or someone.

"Victoria," a deep voice called from the shadows. The man stood tall, wearing an expensive tailored suit that seemed too tight around his shoulders. Tyson. She knew his type all too well—danger wrapped in charm.

She didn't turn around immediately. "I told you we'd meet again when it was time," she replied, her voice smooth like velvet, tinged with a warning.

Tyson approached, a confident smirk crossing his lips as he admired the ruby. "You still got that thing?" he asked, his voice low. "It's a real beauty."

Victoria didn't smile. "Don't get too comfortable," she said, letting the words hang in the air like a warning.

Tyson chuckled, but it was clear there was tension in the room now. Victoria had made her mark, and there was no going back. Tonight would be the start of something bigger, something dangerous. And Tyson would either be part of her plan... or he'd fall like the others.

This gives you a **longer, more detailed opening**, with suspense building slowly and deeper interactions with Victoria's world and the characters around her. As we move forward, I'll make sure to maintain the **high suspense** and the **mystery of each jewel**, while gradually revealing more of her backstory and the dark choices that shaped her.

Let me know if this works for you, and I'll continue expanding the other chapters to fit the desired length and complexity!

CHAPTER 3
Diamond Tongues

Back at her penthouse on Moonview Terrace, Victoria paced the marble floor. The skyline blinked outside her window, a mix of city hope and heavy secrets.

The diamonds around her neck—the ones she'd once hidden inside a false wall in her childhood bedroom—had reappeared when she started getting letters. No return address. Only symbols and hints.

Diamonds, to her, didn't symbolize wealth. They symbolized betrayal. A family member who sold her out. A promise broken under oath. A partner who turned state's witness. Each one carried a name, a memory, and a warning.

She reached into her safe, pulling out an old velvet pouch. Inside, a set of diamond studs. These weren't for fashion. They were the first ones—the ones she wore the night her world flipped upside down.

A knock broke her focus.

It was Marcel, her right hand. Clean-cut. Loyal. Dangerous.

"There's a problem at The Ember Room," he said, not entering until she gave a nod.

"What kind of problem?"

"Someone left a note behind the liquor cabinet. It just said: She's not who you think."

Victoria's eyes narrowed.

Let the games begin.

CHAPTER 4

The Pearl's Whisper

Victoria's heels clicked against the polished marble floor of *Club Ivory*, a members-only lounge tucked deep into the heart of the affluent district of Valemoor—a place no one from her past belonged. The place smelled of old money, jasmine incense, and power deals made over vintage cognac. Her long cream trench coat fluttered as she walked, barely covering the red silk dress that clung to her like sin. Every eye followed her, but she was used to that.

In the corner booth sat a man whose name changed more times than his burner phones. Tonight, he went by *Dixon*, a ghost from her early days—when life still felt raw and survival meant trusting people you'd eventually bury.

"Vic," he nodded, standing slowly, dark suit crisp, silver chain flashing at the collar. "Didn't think you'd show."

She slid into the booth, face unreadable. "Then you don't know me at all."

He poured two glasses of whisky without asking. She didn't touch hers.

"I heard about the Diamond," he said, eyes narrowing.

She kept her expression neutral. "You hear a lot of things."

"The streets are buzzing. Word is, someone's looking for what's theirs. Or what they think is."

She leaned back, lips curling just slightly. "Let them look."

But Dixon's gaze didn't waver. "Pearl told me you might need protection."

At the mention of *Pearl*, Victoria's stomach knotted. That wasn't just a name—it was another jewel, another chapter in the story no one was supposed to read. Pearl had been a friend, a sister in survival, and a liability.

"She's alive?" Victoria asked, voice low.

Dixon gave a slow nod. "Off the grid. Laying low. But she's speaking... to the wrong people."

Victoria's fingers curled around her clutch. "Then she's already dead."

Outside the club, her driver—Malik—was waiting. As they pulled away, Victoria's mind replayed Dixon's words. Pearl. Alive. Talking. That couldn't happen. Not with what she knew.

The car stopped abruptly at a red light, right outside *Luxemart*, a high-end jewelry boutique they used to case years ago when their pockets were empty and their dreams cost too much.

Back then, Pearl wore knock-offs and made them look royal. She'd say, "It's not what's real, it's what they believe." And she believed every gem carried a secret. One night, they stole matching chokers from a private auction—Victoria's lined with diamonds, Pearl's layered with soft, iridescent pearls. Only one got away clean.

Victoria still had hers.

She didn't realize her hand was at her neck until Malik spoke

CHAPTER 5
Diamond Cuts Deep

Victoria didn't flinch. She never did.

Even with Pearl standing just feet away, gun aimed at her like they'd never been sisters in survival.

Pearl's hand trembled slightly, but her eyes—those were steady. Cold. The kind of cold that came from betrayal, heartbreak, and years in hiding.

"You're supposed to be dead," Victoria said flatly, keeping her voice low.

"I was," Pearl replied, stepping closer. "You made sure of it."

Victoria's gaze flicked to the gun, then back to Pearl. "You got the wrong story. I was the one who buried the past, not the people in it."

Pearl's jaw clenched. "Don't get poetic. You left me behind. In Morocco. That fire wasn't an accident, and you know it."

Ah. The Moroccan Opal Job. Victoria had buried more than treasure that night. She'd buried her guilt—and Pearl's screams.

"Why now?" Victoria asked, shifting subtly toward the weight bench. "Why come back after all these years?"

Pearl laughed, a bitter, cracked sound. "Because the Diamond came up for auction again. You remember that one, don't you? The real one. The one we swapped. I tracked it to your last drop in Zurich."

Victoria's stomach tightened. The Zurich switch was years ago, a flawless operation—until it wasn't.

"Someone died for that stone," Pearl continued. "You told me it wasn't real. You said we were just running heat."

"I said what you needed to hear," Victoria snapped. "We were in too deep, and you were sloppy. Always chasing the shine instead of the strategy."

Pearl's finger twitched on the trigger.

"You left me to rot," she whispered. "But guess what? I didn't rot. I evolved. And I've been waiting for the right time to take what's mine."

Victoria took a careful breath. The safehouse was soundproof. No help coming. She needed time—just enough to get inside Pearl's head.

"You think those jewels make you whole?" Victoria asked, voice soft. "They don't. They own you. Every one of them has blood on it. Yours, mine, someone's. You can't wear power and not bleed."

Pearl's eyes shimmered for just a second. Hesitation. Pain. That was the crack Victoria needed.

She lunged. The gun went off—loud, sharp, and deafening in the metal room. Something grazed Victoria's shoulder, but adrenaline pushed her forward. She tackled Pearl, smashing her into the wall.

The gun clattered. They fought like ghosts and gladiators—years of buried rage exploding.

Pearl landed a punch that cracked Victoria's lip. Victoria slammed Pearl against the wall again, holding her by the collar.

"I didn't kill you," Victoria panted. "But I should've."

Pearl shoved her off. "You still might."

Sirens wailed in the distance.

Victoria looked down—Pearl had pressed a hidden panic button on the safe door.

"Who'd you bring?" Victoria hissed.

Pearl's smirk was bloody. "The ones you double-crossed in Zurich. They paid me to lure you out. You're not the only one who makes deals with devils."

Victoria's pulse surged. She grabbed the Diamond and the Pearl from the case and bolted for the back exit. Gunfire shattered the silence as masked men stormed the building.

She ran—heels discarded, coat torn, jewels tucked into her bra.

Malik's car screeched around the corner.

She dove in. "Drive. Now."

"Where to?" he asked.

She didn't hesitate. "We need to disappear. New names. New city. But first..." she looked at the blood on her arm, the

Diamond glowing under her torn blouse, "...we go to Jasper Hill. That's where it all began. And that's where we finish it."

As the city faded behind them, Victoria knew the hunt was just beginning.

Because Pearl wasn't the only ghost. And the Diamond wasn't the only secret.

And if the past was catching up—
She was ready to cut deeper.

CHAPTER 6
Blood On Jasper Hill

Jasper Hill wasn't a place. It was a wound.

An old mining town turned ghost district just outside of Halifax, it sat abandoned on the edge of Canada like a warning. Victoria hadn't been there in over twelve years—not since the first heist. Not since the day she became someone else.

The gravel crunched under Malik's tires as they pulled up to the rusting gates. A faded sign read:
NO ENTRY – PROPERTY OF THE COMMONWEALTH
But nothing about Victoria Blair had ever been common.

"This is where it started?" Malik asked, eyeing the decaying buildings beyond the gate.

"Before I was Victoria," she said. "This is where I was Vivica Cross."

She stepped out, the wind cutting like a blade. Jasper Hill held a darkness that was both spiritual and personal. The kind that stuck to your skin.

Malik followed her through the breach in the fence. "You sure we're not being tracked?"

She glanced over her shoulder. "If we are, they'll regret it."

The old refinery was half-collapsed, its tower leaning like a warning finger pointed at the sky. Inside, the air was thick with rust and regret.

Victoria led Malik to a locker buried behind collapsed beams. She cracked it open with a crowbar.

Inside:

A box of old passports

A rusted gun

A photograph of four women—her, Pearl, and two others now long dead

And a velvet pouch

She opened it.

Four rough-cut gems spilled into her palm. Raw. Unpolished. Worth millions—if not for the curse they carried. Each gem was linked to a different betrayal. Each one had been soaked in blood.

"I thought you were after the Diamond," Malik said.

"I am," she said. "But this... this was the real job. We stole these from a Russian tycoon who bought up Jasper Hill for illegal mining. The diamonds were never legal. We were supposed to sell them and vanish. But Pearl kept the fourth stone. I buried the others."

"And the tycoon?" he asked.

She didn't answer.

A sudden snap of branches outside made them freeze.

Victoria pulled the rusted gun from the locker and signaled for silence.

Footsteps. One. Two. Then nothing.

Until a voice echoed from the shadows:
"Vivica... You always did love your souvenirs."

Victoria raised the gun. "Show yourself."

A man emerged, tall and elegant, with eyes like black ice and a scar down his right cheek.

"Dmitri," she said, voice a whisper. "I watched you fall off that cliff."

"You should've stayed to make sure I hit the bottom."

Malik stepped forward, but Victoria held him back. Dmitri Petrov had once been the fifth member of their crew—and her lover. The one she betrayed for Pearl.

He held up a black briefcase. "I'm not here for revenge. I'm here to trade."

Victoria narrowed her eyes. "Trade what?"

He opened the briefcase. Inside, a necklace gleamed: a sapphire teardrop surrounded by black diamonds.

"The Ocean's Eye," she breathed.

"Pearl gave it to me," Dmitri said. "She said to bring it here. Said it belonged to you."

Victoria's face darkened. Pearl wasn't just playing with the past—she was rewriting it.

"I don't trust you," Victoria said.

"Neither do I," Dmitri said. "But I know where she's going next. And if you want to stop her, you'll need me."

Victoria clenched the velvet pouch tighter. "You double-cross me again, Dmitri..."

He smiled. "Darling, isn't that how we started?"

She turned to Malik. "We leave in ten. I need to bury what's left of Vivica before Victoria finishes what she started."

As they walked away from the refinery, Malik asked the question sitting in the air between them.

"What exactly did Pearl steal from you?"

Victoria didn't pause. "My name. My lover. My life. And the last jewel."

He waited.

She looked him dead in the eye.
"She took the one I swore I'd never lose—The Heartstone. And if she activates it, everything burns."

CHAPTER 7
The Vault In Velvet Hollow

Velvet Hollow was neither velvet nor hollow.
It was a private club hidden underneath an abandoned
opera house in Montreal. From the outside, the building
was crumbling—a forgotten relic of another time. But
underground, it pulsed with power, secrets, and
everything illegal money could buy.

Victoria stood outside the iron door, dressed in sleek black, her face shadowed by a tilted fedora. Malik adjusted the cufflink cam on his sleeve and whispered into her ear, "You sure Pearl's inside?"

"She's drawn to places like this. Secretive. Expensive. Dangerous," Victoria replied. "It's not about the jewels anymore. She's building something bigger."

"What's bigger than blood diamonds?"

"Control," Victoria said flatly. "And I think she's about to auction off the key."

They stepped inside. The music was a slow jazz number, smoky and hypnotic. The crowd was a blend of elite criminals, politicians with too much immunity, and ghosts of old power.

All eyes turned when Victoria entered. She didn't flinch. She moved like she owned the room—and once, she had.

A woman in crimson approached. She was tall, with shaved sides, emerald lipstick, and tattoos that told a violent story.

"Victoria Blair," she said, offering a poisoned smile. "Or should I say... Vivica."

"I'm who I need to be," Victoria said, locking eyes with her. "Where's Pearl?"

"She's backstage. But you'll need more than a name to get through. You'll need *currency*."

Victoria held up a single black diamond. The room paused. People knew what it meant.

The woman stepped aside.

Malik leaned in. "What *was* that?"

"One of the Lost Nine. They're keys to inner sanctums. And death warrants."

Backstage, the air shifted. It smelled of money, powder, and revenge.

There was a stage. Velvet curtains. And in the center, encased in laser glass: *The Heartstone.*

It was flawless. Cut into the shape of a flame. Red like blood and ancient in aura.

Pearl stood beside it.

She wore silver and shame like perfume. Her smile was wicked and soft.

"Victoria," she purred. "You look *almost* like someone I used to love."

"You took what wasn't yours," Victoria said, stepping closer.

Pearl tilted her head. "And you *left* what you didn't understand."

The room filled with tension. Behind them, doors locked. Guards flanked the exits.

This was no auction. It was a *trap*.

Pearl tapped the glass, and the Heartstone began to glow.

"The stone doesn't just unlock vaults," Pearl said. "It amplifies energy. Memories. Rage. And secrets. You and I... we were always going to end here."

Victoria didn't blink. "Then end it."

Pearl nodded toward the ceiling. The chandelier above Victoria shattered, crashing to the floor. Chaos erupted. Malik dove forward, tackling one of the guards. Smoke grenades hissed.

In the frenzy, Pearl vanished through a hidden corridor behind the stage.

Victoria gave chase, bullets flying past her head. She turned a corner—empty. Just walls of velvet.

Until a voice whispered, "You still don't know what you're running from."

She spun. No one.

But a small envelope lay on the floor. Sealed with wax. She opened it.

Inside, a single photograph: Victoria and Pearl, years ago, holding the Heartstone together—and behind them, someone Victoria had forgotten.

Her mother.
Alive.
And smiling beside Pearl.

CHAPTER 8
The Woman In The Photograph

Victoria stared at the photograph as if it had slapped her.

Her mother—alive. Standing shoulder-to-shoulder with
Pearl, wearing that same necklace Victoria once buried after
the funeral. It was impossible. Her mother died in a fire.
Closed casket. Government documents. Grief counselors.

And yet here she was.

Smiling. Beside Pearl. Holding the Heartstone like it belonged to her.

Malik caught up, blood on his knuckles and panic in his eyes. "What happened? Are you hit?"

Victoria handed him the photo, her voice low and shaking. "Look."

He examined it, then looked up, stunned. "Is this—?"

"Yes," Victoria whispered. "And I don't understand."

Malik moved her behind a pillar as more guards swept the halls. "Maybe it's a fake. Maybe it's a warning."

"She wouldn't fake my mother. Pearl knows what she's doing. She's been ten steps ahead this whole time."

Malik paused. "If your mom's alive... it means she lied to you your whole life. Or someone lied for her."

The silence between them weighed a ton.

Victoria replayed every childhood memory, every bedtime story, every Sunday morning where her mother hummed gospel songs and braided her hair. None of it made sense anymore.

They escaped Velvet Hollow through a trap door behind the dressing room. It led into old sewer tunnels that ran underneath the city. Malik hacked the electrical box to short the security grid, and they slipped away like ghosts.

Later, at a safehouse in a fictional town called Ashmont Reach, Victoria sat on a wooden crate under a flickering light. A whiskey bottle stood untouched beside her. She wasn't ready to drink—not while the truth was burning through her chest.

She unrolled the scroll Pearl had left with the photo.

There were blueprints. Not of a building—but of a machine.

A blueprint designed by "B. Blair."

Her mother's signature.

"It's a frequency amplifier," Malik explained, eyes scanning the document. "Looks like something that could boost the Heartstone's power across city grids. Maybe even control... people."

Victoria blinked. "Control...?"

"Think hypnosis, but bigger. Like mass obedience. Anyone who wears a certain frequency—maybe in jewelry, maybe implants—they'd be theirs."

Victoria stood, hands on her hips. "So this was never about the jewels. This was about power. Control. Dominion."

"And your mother... was in on it," Malik said quietly.

Or worse, Victoria thought—she started it.

Her hands shook. Not from fear. From fury.

"They've underestimated me," she said.

"What now?"

She lit the blueprint on fire. "Now, we go to Stonehill. That's where my mother was last seen before she 'died.' Pearl's trail leads there."

As the paper turned to ash, Victoria whispered to herself, "We're not just chasing stones. We're chasing ghosts."

And for the first time in years, Victoria wasn't afraid of what she'd find.

She was ready.

CHAPTER 9

Stonehill

Stonehill wasn't on any real map. A ghost town nestled in the forested cliffs past Ashmont Reach, known only by whispers and coordinates passed between jewel smugglers and rogue scientists.

Victoria and Malik arrived just before dawn. Fog clung to the broken signs and gutted buildings like a veil hiding sins. One building stood out—an old cathedral retrofitted with solar panels, chain-linked fences, and biometric locks.

"That's where the signal is strongest," Malik said, scanning a handheld reader. "Your mother's blueprints were being implemented *here*."

Victoria's heartbeat was a war drum. "Then that's where we go."

They broke in through a shattered stained-glass window. The scent inside was a blend of metal, ozone, and burning sage. Technology and spirituality—two things that had no business being fused, yet here they were, twisted together in one unholy lab.

Inside, monitors flickered with footage of major cities: Westbyne, Klenwood, even Larchmere—the town Victoria grew up in. Her childhood street, now surveilled in real-time.

"They've mapped the whole city grid," Malik whispered. "Every citizen wearing a Heartstone variant is... traceable. Influenceable."

Victoria turned to the largest screen, where an image blinked into focus.

Her mother.

Not in a lab coat. Not in disguise.

In full leadership mode—standing behind a podium emblazoned with the logo of *The Echelon*, a fabricated political movement the world hadn't heard of yet.

"She's preparing to *launch*," Malik muttered. "Mass activation. If she uses that frequency—"

"She'll own them all," Victoria finished. "Free will, gone."

As they dug deeper into the control room, they discovered a chamber—cold, glass-walled, humming with low-frequency energy. Inside were mannequins wearing various jewelry designs, all pulsing faintly.

Heartstone variants.

A prototype bracelet sparked. Its tag read: "**GEN-5: Crowd Sync Beta.**"

Suddenly, a voice echoed from above.

"You never were one to stay buried, Victoria."

She spun around.

Her mother.

Alive. Regal. Unapologetic.

Dressed in all black, her fingers adorned with rings housing shimmering stones. She looked untouched by time, as if pain couldn't find her.

"You left me!" Victoria yelled.

"I protected you," her mother said coldly. "I kept you out of this. But you kept digging."

"Because lies rot in silence. You *lied* about everything. About Dad. About the stones. About who you *are*."

Her mother walked down the steps slowly. "I *am* your mother. And I am also the architect of a new era. These people don't want freedom—they want *direction*. And I'm going to give it to them."

Victoria shook her head. "Through control?"

"Through *order*."

"And if I resist?"

Her mother paused. "Then you'll become my greatest threat."

Malik pulled Victoria back as guards swarmed in.

Victoria's voice didn't waver. "You'll need more than stones to stop me."

They escaped through the fire tunnels beneath the cathedral, dodging bullets and betrayal.

Once safe under the cover of dusk, Malik said, "You still want to go after her?"

Victoria didn't hesitate.

"She trained me to lead. She just didn't expect I'd lead a *rebellion*."

CHAPTER 10
Frequencies Don't Lie

Victoria stood inside the Safehouse vault in Old Jerico, the encrypted hideout where rogue scientists and truth-smugglers gathered to dismantle dangerous tech. Malik sat across from her, bruised but alive. The data cube retrieved from Stonehill glowed on the table, pulsing like a heartbeat.

"I decrypted what we stole," he said. "There's more. Your mother's not just launching in one city."

Victoria leaned in. "Where else?"

"Every major city with Heartstone tech—North Terrin, Vysana, Port Maxwell, and yes... even what's left of Klenwood. Tonight."

A map projected above the cube, red dots blinking like silent alarms across the globe. She watched them connect—*a network of control, disguised as empowerment.*

"This is no jewelry line," Victoria whispered. "It's an *empire*."

Malik nodded. "And she's already activated a soft phase. People are reporting blackouts, blank stares, personality flips."

Victoria clenched her jaw. "The Gen-5 bracelet. Crowd Sync."

The bracelet she once wore now felt like a curse tattooed on memory.

Suddenly, the cube beeped.

A message played.

Not from her mother—but from *her father*.

His voice.

"If you're seeing this, it means I'm dead—or worse. Victoria, your mother and I began this project together. But she turned it dark. I tried to stop her. That's why I disappeared."

The screen flickered to his lab journal, dated six years earlier. He had tried to develop a *counter-frequency*—one that could disable the influence of the stones. But his last entry was incomplete.

Victoria stood, staring at the formula fragments and code lines. "He left me the key."

Malik stared. "You sure you want to go back in?"

"She raised a soldier. But she also made a strategist."

Victoria uploaded the data to her palm drive. "We go to *Nova Circuit*. That's where the main frequency tower is."

Hours Later – Nova Circuit

The tower was a gleaming monolith at the city's edge—futuristic, cloaked in a fake charity front. Inside, Victoria climbed through ducts, bypassed lasers, and reached the core room.

Guards surrounded the mainboard. A trigger countdown read: **00:23:59**.

She slid behind the control panel. Malik tapped furiously, inputting her father's broken code.

Sweat dripped down Victoria's spine.

"Ten seconds," Malik whispered.

A voice called out behind her.

"Don't," her mother said, stepping into the room, calm and cruel. "You'll trigger mass instability. You'll *kill* them."

Victoria's hand hovered over the enter key.

"You already *did*," she replied.

Malik hit enter.

The system flashed. Error. Override.

The screens glitched—

Then... the Heartstone network *crashed.*

City by city, jewelry blinked out. People collapsed, some screaming, some unconscious. Others... just stared, dazed.

The transmission halted.

Silence.

Her mother screamed. "You stupid girl!"

Victoria turned. "I learned from the best."

Two Days Later

Victoria sat on a rooftop overlooking Klenwood. News channels were flooded with stories of mass awakenings, strange jewelry malfunctions, and a sudden blackout in cities linked to the Heartstone movement.

Her comm buzzed.

Incoming Message: UNMARKED NUMBER

"You stopped the tower. But not the roots. This isn't over. It never was."

Attached was a video.

A lab. A man. Her father?

But this man *looked* different.

Alive.

Only one word played from the video, before it cut to static.
"Run."

Final Quote from Victoria:

"The world thinks truth is gold. But the real jewels? They're buried in the lies we survive."

Acknowledgments

Ac ut consequat semper viverra nam libero justo laoreet sit. Adipiscing tristique risus nec feugiat in. Nulla posuere sollicitudin aliquam ultrices sagittis orci a scelerisque. Ultricies lacus sed turpis tincidunt id aliquet risus feugiat in. Ullamcorper eget nulla facilisi etiam dignissim diam quis. Purus in mollis nunc sed id semper risus. Accumsan sit amet nulla facilisi morbi tempus iaculis urna.

www.ingramcontent.com/pod-product-compliance
Lightning Source LLC
Chambersburg PA
CBHW071228130626
46555CB00004B/1891